By Don Hoffman
Illustrated by Todd Dakins

P corn
PRESS™

Affiliated Publishers
Milwaukee • Denver • Vancouver, B.C.

Cover Design and Illustrations by Todd Dakins
Text Design by Shelby Keefe

04   03   02   01   00   5   4   3   2   1

ISBN: 0-9702518-0-7
Library of Congress Catalog Card Number: 00-103621
First Printing September 2000
Printed in Korea

Published by Popcorn Press, a division of Printstar Books, Milwaukee, Wisconsin

5630 N. Lake Drive, Milwaukee, Wisconsin 53217
414-906-0600 • e-mail: pbpub@execpc.com

Affiliated Publishers
Milwaukee • Denver • Vancouver, B.C.

Thank you from the children of *Sam's Hope:*

100 Black Men; Agape Community Center; Andrus, Sceales, Starke & Sawall; Barnes & Noble; BORDERS Books, Music, & Cafe; Brady Corporation; Burton & Mayer; CBS 58; Cd & Lee; Chocolate House; community and private donors; Congregation Shalom; Creative Works; Todd Dakins; Festival City Symphony; Firstar Bank; Futech; Gareth Stevens Publishing; Garner Family Fund; Don Hoffman; Harry W. Schwartz Bookshops; Incentive Gallery; Lands' End; The Learning Shop; Legacy Bank; Lorraine and Morry Mitz Charitable Foundation; Marcus Theatres Corporation; Marquette University; McManus Family Fund; Milwaukee Brewers; Milwaukee Bucks; Milwaukee Rampage; Popcorn Press; Printstar Books; Reunions Magazine; Rosalie Manor Community & Family Services; SHARE; Regina & Stanford Sloves; Starbucks Coffee Company; Uihlein Soccer Park; Wepco Printing; youth groups; and public and private schools.

To grant the gift of literacy call **414-351-2949, e-mail us at samshope@execpc.com or visit our website at www.samshope.org**

To my mom, who was never too busy to find time to read to me each day.
It always made me feel so special.

And to Sam's Hope, who helps the little Billys out there realize their
"big boy" dream of someday being able to read.

To God and my family

TODD

Today is Billy's birthday. Today it is true.

Today Billy is a big boy. Are you a big boy too?

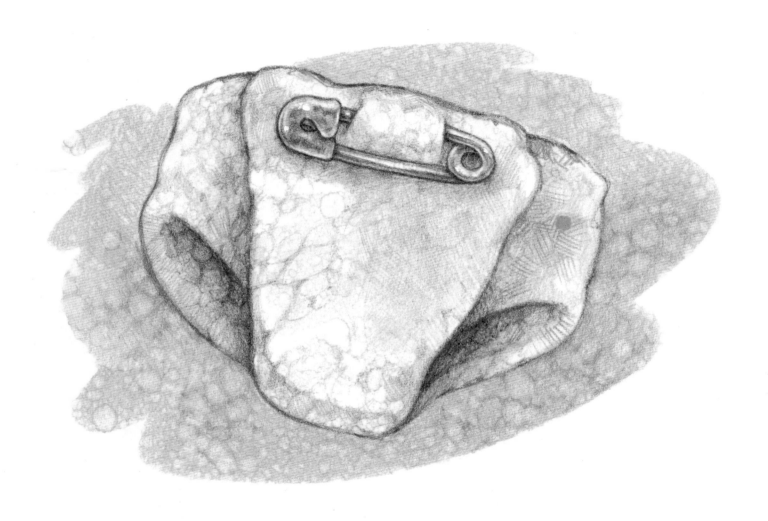

Billy used to wear diapers.

Now he wears underpants. Billy is a big boy.
How about you? Do you wear underpants? Are you a big boy too?

Billy used to have a bottle.

Now he uses a cup. Billy is a big boy.
How about you? Do you use a cup? Are you a big boy too?

Billy used to use a potty chair.

Now he uses the toilet. Billy is a big boy.
How about you? Do you use the toilet? Are you a big boy too?

Billy used to take baby baths.

Now he uses the shower. Billy is a big boy.
How about you? Do you use the shower? Are you a big boy too?

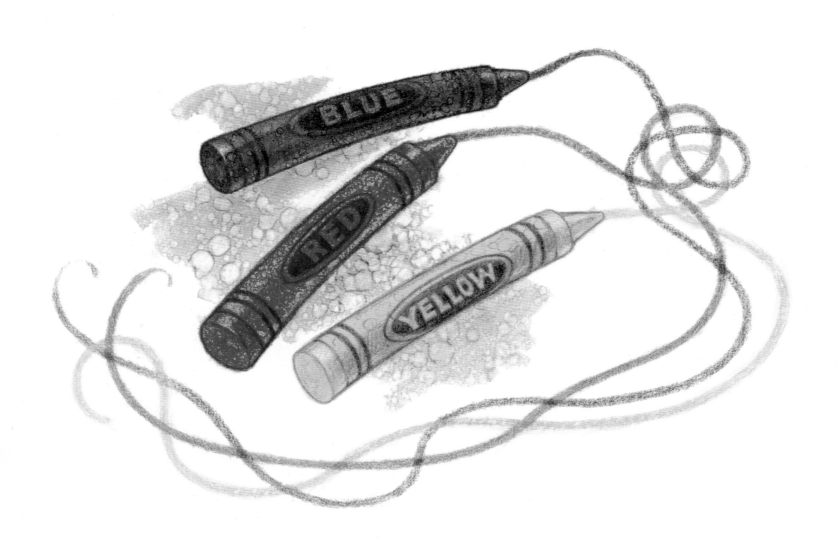

Billy used to print with crayons.

Now he writes with a pencil. Billy is a big boy.
How about you? Do you write with a pencil? Are you a big boy too?

Billy used to talk baby talk.

Now he knows his ABCs. Billy is a big boy.
How about you? Do you know your ABCs? Are you a big boy too?

Billy used to use a high chair.

Now he uses a booster seat. Billy is a big boy.
How about you? Do you use a booster seat? Are you a big boy too?

Billy used to wear slip-on shoes.

Now he knows how to tie his laces. Billy is a big boy. How about you?
Do you know how to tie your laces? Are you a big boy too?

Billy used to ride a tricycle.

Now he knows how to ride a bike. Billy is a big boy. How about you?
Do you know how to ride a bike? Are you a big boy too?

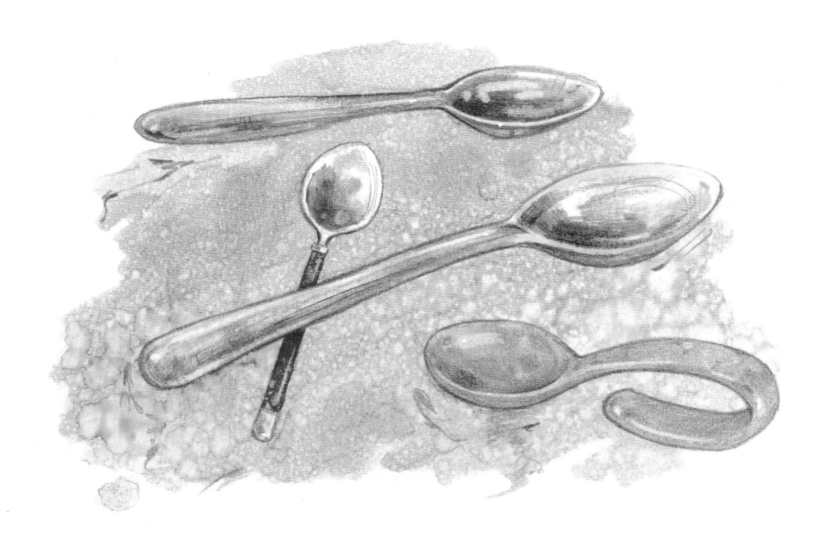

Billy used to eat with only a spoon.

Now he knows how to use a fork. Billy is a big boy. How about you?
Do you know how to use a fork? Are you a big boy too?

Billy used to have a pacifier.

Now he has a lollipop. Billy is a big boy.
How about you? Do you have a lollipop? Are you a big boy too?

Billy used to ride in a car seat.

Now he knows how to buckle his seat belt. Billy is a big boy.
How about you? Do you know how to buckle your seat belt?
Are you a big boy too?

Can you picture it? Can it be true?

Billy is a big boy.

Now YOU are a big boy too!